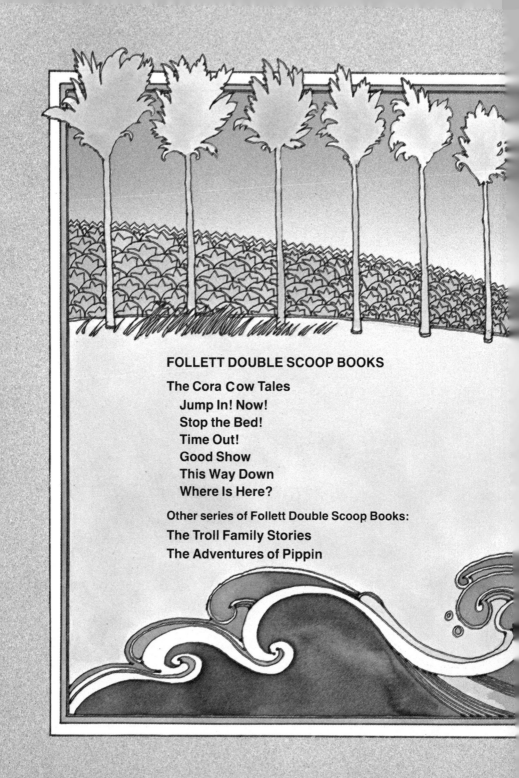

FOLLETT DOUBLE SCOOP BOOKS

The Cora Cow Tales
  Jump In! Now!
  Stop the Bed!
  Time Out!
  Good Show
  This Way Down
  Where Is Here?

Other series of Follett Double Scoop Books:
The Troll Family Stories
The Adventures of Pippin

JUMP IN! NOW!

**Phylliss Adams
Eleanore Hartson
Mark Taylor**

Illustrated by John Sandford

Follett Publishing Company
Chicago, Illinois

Atlanta, Georgia · Dallas, Texas
Sacramento, California · Warrensburg, Missouri

LC 81-71351
ISBN 0-695-41645-6
ISBN 0-695-31645-1 (pbk.)

"What a good day!" said Cora Cow.
"I love it here."

"Mary and I are going to
play ball now," said Will Berg.
"Do you want to play, Cora?"

"No," said Cora.
"I am going to read.
But you two have fun."

"This is fun," Mary said to Will.
"I like this game."

"Look out, Mary," said Will.
"Get the ball. Run fast."

Mary ran fast.
But she did not get the ball.

The ball went all the way to
a big rock.
Mary and Will went to get the ball.
But they were afraid of the waves.
So they got up on the big rock.

"Help! Help!" called Mary and Will.

Cora looked up.

She saw Mary and Will on the rock.

Cora jumped up fast.

"Here I come," said Cora.
"Cora to the rescue!"

"Jump in this," said Cora.

"In that thing?" Mary said.

"Yes, in this thing," said Cora.
"Jump in! Now!"

"Here we go!" Cora said.
"Do not be afraid.
This will be a fast ride."

Cora went fast.

"Did you see Cora?" said Will.
"She came to the rescue."

"I saw Cora," said Mr. Berg.
"She is <u>some</u> cow!"

"Thank you, Cora. Thank you!"
said Mr. Berg.

"We love you, Cora," said Mary and Will.

"And I love you, too," said Mrs. Berg.

"What a day!" said Cora.

"What a rescue!" said Mary.

"And what a cow!" laughed Will.

Ride the Waves to Cora

Start at the rock.
Now find a yellow boat.
Go to the green turtle.
Find the red ball.
Get on the blue fish.
Now ride the waves to Cora.

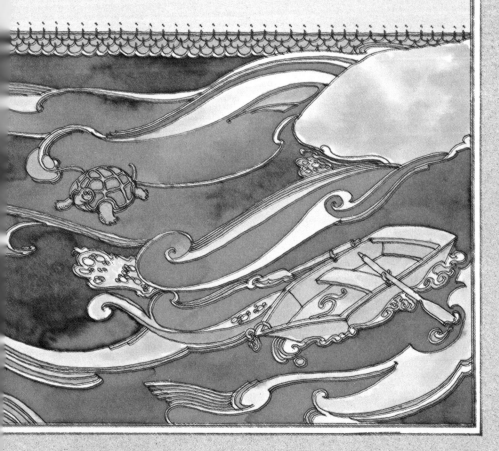

Tell Why

Cora is wet. Why?

Cora is thanking the girl. Why?

Cora is happy. Why?

Cora is laughing. Why?

What Happened?

Look at each picture.
What happened first?
What happened next?
What happened last?

All the words that appear in the story *Jump In! Now!*
are listed here.

a	fast	Mary	thank
afraid	fun	Mr. Berg	that
all		Mrs. Berg	the
am	game		they
and	get	no	thing
are	go	not	this
	good	now	to
ball	got		too
be		of	two
big	have	on	
but	help	out	up
	here		
called		play	want
came	I		waves
come	in	ran	way
Cora Cow	is	read	we
cow	it	rescue	went
		ride	were
day	jump	rock	what
did	laughed	run	will
do	like		
	look	said	yes
	love	saw	you
		see	
		she	
		so	
		some	

About the Authors

Phylliss Adams, Eleanore Hartson, and Mark Taylor have a
combined background that includes writing books for children
and teachers, teaching at the elementary and university
levels, and working in the areas of curriculum development,
reading instruction and research, teacher training, parent
education, and library and media services.

About the Illustrator

Since attending the American Academy of Art in Chicago,
Illinois, John Sandford has concentrated on illustration for
books and magazines.
  The artist works in Chicago, where he lives with
his wife, Frances. The illustrations for Cora Cow were
executed in the spirit of the artist's father, who left
to the Sandford family the rich legacy of his creativity.

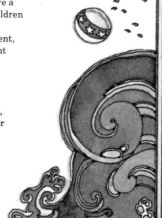